Clogpots in Space

Scoular Anderson

Collins

Best Friends • Jessy and the Bridesmaid's Dress •
Jessy Runs Away • **Rachel Anderson**
Changing Charlie • Clogpots in Space • **Scoular Anderson**
Ernest the Heroic Lion-tamer • Ivana the Inventor • **Damon Burnard**
Two Hoots • **Helen Cresswell**
Magic Mash • Nina's Machines • **Peter Firmin**
Shadows on the Barn • **Sarah Garland**
Clever Trevor • The Mystery of Lydia Dustbin's Diamonds • Nora Bone •
Nora Bone and the Tooth Fairy • **Brough Girling**
Sharon and Darren • **Nigel Gray**
Thing-in-a-Box • Thing-on-Two-Legs • **Diana Hendry**
Desperate for a Dog • More Dog Trouble • **Rose Impey**
Georgie and the Dragon • Georgie and the Planet Raider • **Julia Jarman**
Cowardy Cowardy Cutlass • Cutlass Rules the Waves • Free With Every Pack •
Mo and the Mummy Case • The Fizziness Business • **Robin Kingsland**
And Pigs Might Fly! • Albertine, Goose Queen • Jigger's Day Off •
Martians at Mudpuddle Farm • Mossop's Last Chance •
Mum's the Word • **Michael Morpurgo**
Granny Grimm's Gruesome Glasses • **Jenny Nimmo**
Grubble Trouble • **Hilda Offen**
Hiccup Harry • Harry Moves House • Harry's Party • Harry the Superhero •
Harry with Spots On • **Chris Powling**
Grandad's Concrete Garden • **Shoo Rayner**
Rattle and Hum – Robot Detectives • **Frank Rodgers**
Our Toilet's Haunted • **John Talbot**
Pesters of the West • **Lisa Taylor**
Lost Property • **Pat Thomson**
Monty the Dog Who Wears Glasses • Monty Bites Back • Monty Ahoy! •
Monty Must Be Magic! • Monty – Up To His Neck in Trouble! • **Colin West**
Ging Gang Goolie, It's an Alien • **Bob Wilson**

First published in Great Britain by
A & C Black (Publishers) Ltd 1994
First published by Collins 1994
10 9 8 7 6 5 4

Collins is an imprint of HarperCollins Children's Books part of
HarperCollins Publishers Ltd. 77-85 Fulham Palace Road, London W6 8JB

Text and illustrations copyright © 1994 Scoular Anderson
All rights reserved.

ISBN 0-00-674848 1

Printed in Great Britain by
Clays Ltd, St Ives plc

CHAPTER 1

Dexter Clogpot and his big brother
Bernie were watching a horror film
on TV . . .

It was about two space-travellers stranded on the planet Snirv.

One of the space travellers was about to be eaten by horrible green slimy Snirvians when suddenly . . .

. . . weird hands slithered round
Bernie's neck.

It was Dexter's and Bernie's sister,
Rosabella.

She had just come
back from the
local jumble sale.

They all trooped outside.

Rosabella opened up the back of
their van . . .

. . . and pulled out . . .

Rosabella could see the boys were disappointed.

CHAPTER 2

The Clogpots weren't very brainy.
But they could work things out
slowly, and Bernie's brain had
started to tick.

Then, Dexter went off to the hire-shop and came back with the proper machine for blowing up hot-air balloons.

At first the balloon wriggled.

Then it twitched.

Then it began to grow . . .

and grow . . .

and grow . . .

and grow . . .

Until . . .

Dexter

caught hold

of Blinko

just before

the basket

left the ground.

Then up they floated.

To begin with, it was quite exciting.
They had a good view of their town,
Muddyflatts . . .

. . . and the countryside . . .

. . . and the sea.

Bernie looked around. He had never driven a balloon before.

But by now the sun was setting and it was getting dark.

The Clogpots were so tired after their exciting day that they fell asleep.

Dexter woke first.
It was very cold
and dark.

For a moment he wondered why the
rest of the family was curled up
beside him. Then he remembered.

He peered over the side of the
basket . . .

. . . and saw an
amazing sight.

He woke Rosabella and Bernie.

When all the Clogpots were awake
they stared out of the basket.

We've
floated
right up
into space!

Rosabella was in no mood for excuses.

Bernie thought.

Then something nearby caught
his eye.

Bernie found an
extra piece of rope
lying in the
bottom of the
basket.

He made it
into a lasso.

Then he threw it . . .

. . . several times . . .

. . . until he caught the satellite.

33

Dexter began to climb
across. The rope
swung and sagged.

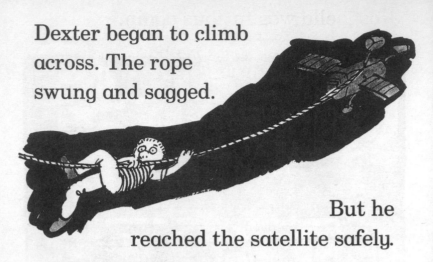

But he
reached the satellite safely.

As he jumped
for joy the
satellite gave
a creak and
began to move
away from the basket.

In a few seconds, Dexter and his
satellite had disappeared into the
blackness of outer space.

Rosabella was furious again.

And Rosabella sat down for a really good cry.

Meanwhile, back in Muddyflatts,
Mr Plummer was opening up his
planetarium for the day.

He was feeling pleased with himself.
The planetarium had just been
repainted and Mr Plummer had
installed a new control panel.

SHOWS
AT
2.15 pm
and
4.15 pm
DAILY

CAFÉ

ICES

PLUMMER'S PLANETARIUM
special lighting
and sound effects
now installed
· ·
Experience a
life-like and
educational voyage
round the solar
system!

He was tidying up the litter round the door.

When he noticed a large piece of red and green material hanging down the wall.

Mr Plummer was so short-sighted, he didn't notice that the piece of material was hanging from a ventilator shaft on the roof.

I'll get Mr Smarmly to deal with it.

There were one or two other things that Mr Plummer didn't know that afternoon.

He didn't know that the Clogpots' hot-air balloon had fallen down his ventilator shaft.

He didn't know that Mrs Todpole was stealing money from the cash box and hiding it away.

He didn't know that Mr Smarmly made faces behind his back.

He didn't know that the dentist was
Mr Smarmly's cousin.

Mr Plummer didn't know just how
exciting it was going to be.

CHAPTER 6

As soon as Mr Plummer
had gone, Mr Smarmly
puffed out his puny
chest,

I'm in
charge
now!

and bossed Mrs Todpole around.

Remember we're
letting the public
in at
2 pm
exactly.

I _know_ that.

TICKETS

Stuck-up
stick
insect!

Mr Smarmly crept upstairs. He wasn't allowed in the control room, but today he could sneak in and have a look.

He sat in Mr Plummer's seat and spread his hands over the control panel.

He imagined himself bringing up the lights on the planet Saturn. The audience would go "OOOH!' He imagined talking into the microphone.

He got up, walked into the planetarium and gazed up at the planets hanging in the dimness. Then a shiver ran down his spine. He could hear strange noises.

Mr Smarmly strained his ears. Yes,
he could hear strange sounds . . .

MUNCH
MUNCH
MUNCH

Rosabella had
found a bar of chocolate in her bag.
She and Bernie were munching it,
sitting in the bottom of the basket
while they decided what to do.

. . . very strange sounds . . .
SNIFF
SNIFF
PAD PAD
Blinko had gone exploring.

. . . sounds he had never heard
before in the planetarium.
Really creepy sounds.

GROAN!

Dexter had fallen
off his satellite.

Just as Mr Smarmly was about to
turn on all the lights, Mrs Todpole
called him.

Oh, Mr
Smarmleeee!

She was selling tickets.

Of course he hadn't returned, he
was still with Mr Smarmly's cousin,
the dentist.

CHAPTER **7**

People were taking their seats in the planetarium.

PLUMMER'S PLANETARIUM

Mr Smarmly went into the control room.

TICKETS

In a few moments he would raise
the curtains.

He would press buttons and flick
switches. Planets and stars would
move about on unseen wires and
pulleys.

Mr Smarmly switched on the lights
and turned up the music.
The show had begun.

On the TV monitor, Mr Smarmly
noticed that something wasn't
right.

He told himself it was just his
imagination.

Mr Smarmly tried to calm himself,

but he could hear the audience
laughing. Things were going
very wrong.

Mr Smarmly dashed out of the
control room to see what was
happening . . .

. . . just as Dexter crept in.

There had been lots of noise. He
had heard music and laughter.
One minute it was dark, then
lights went on and
off again. He had
fallen from a great
height. Now he
was confused.

Dexter began to press buttons and flick switches.

While Dexter
was trying to
work out how to
fly a spacecraft . . .

. . . Mr Smarmly
was trying to get
along a corridor . . .

. . . filled with
bits and pieces
left by the
workmen . . .

. . . when they
were doing up the
planetarium.

Then Dexter heard loud cheers.

He decided to go out.

Mr Plummer had arrived just as the performance was starting. He had never seen anything quite like it.

Earlier in the day there were lots of things that Mr Plummer didn't know. Now he knew . . .

. . . about Mr Smarmly

and Mrs Todpole . . .

. . . and the Clogpots.
The way the Clogpots had found
themselves in outer-space was the
funniest thing he had ever heard.

He gave Mr Smarmly and
Mrs Todpole the sack. But he
kept the Clogpots.

'Well,' said Rosabella . . .

'. . . who would have thought a visit to the jumble sale would end up like this!'